# The Snow Queen

Retold by Susanna Davidson

Illustrated by Elena Selivanova

Long ago and far away, there were two best friends, Gerda and Kay.

In summer, they grew roses in their window boxes...

...in winter, they gathered around the fire.
Kay's grandmother told them stories of the wicked
Snow Queen, who had a frozen heart of ice.

Then, one cold, dark night,
Kay glimpsed the Snow Queen.

With tiny shards of ice, she
pierced his eye and heart.

And after that, he changed.

Everything that once
looked beautiful to him
now seemed mean and ugly.

The winter grew colder. The Snow Queen rode into town on her silver sleigh. "Come with me," she called to Kay.

Entranced, he climbed aboard. In a flurry of snowflakes, she swept him away.

All winter, Gerda longed
for her friend's return.

At the first sign of spring, she followed the flow of the river to find him.

On she sailed, past gardens blooming with roses,

past woods and meadows,

and waterbirds that ducked and dived in the reeds.

The boat came to rest on a rocky shore, far from home. A raven hopped out to greet her.

"I know of Kay," cawed the raven. "He lives in a palace with a princess. I will take you to him."

As night fell, they arrived at the palace,
thick with the shadows of dreams.

In the topmost tower, two petal beds hung from
a golden stem – one white, one scarlet.

"Kay!" cried Gerda. The boy awoke,
turned his head... but it was not Kay.

"Oh!" sobbed Gerda. Through falling tears, she told her story.

"We will help you find your friend," said the princess.

"Take our golden coach to speed you on your way."

The coach rolled across fields and into a tangled forest.
There, a band of robbers spied its glinting gold.

Out they rushed. They seized the horses and rode the coach hard and fast to their castle.

"Let me go," pleaded Gerda. But a little robber girl clung to her. "Stay here and be my playmate."

Gerda shook her head. "I must find my friend Kay," she said.

That night, the birds looked down from the rafters.

"Coo, coo, coo," they sang. "We have seen little Kay."

"He has gone with the Snow Queen to Lapland, far away in the frozen north."

At dawn, while the robbers snored in their sleep, the little robber girl called for Ba, her reindeer.

"I'll not keep you here," she said. "Go! Find your friend. Ba will take you to Lapland. He knows the way."

And she gave Gerda a thick shawl to wear, and a bag filled with parcels of bread and meat.

Away Ba flew, over bush and briar, over moor and heath, as fast as he could go.

There are the northern lights. See how they flicker and glow.

On they sped, faster and faster, day and night. The loaves of bread were gone, and the meat too; and now they were in Lapland.

They took shelter from the cold with an
old woman, who warmed them by her fire.

"You still have a hundred miles to go," she said,
"before you reach the Snow Queen's palace."

"And there, it is true, you will find your friend, Kay."

"You are in luck:
the Snow Queen is
away, bringing cold to
southern lands...

...but she has already
enchanted Kay.

He will never escape
unless you can melt
the ice in his heart."

It was the last of the journey now. The biting wind tore at them, icy and strong. In the shadow of the Snow Queen's palace, Ba stopped and bowed his head. "I cannot go on," he said.

Bravely, Gerda went on alone. The Snow Queen's guards surrounded her – living snowflakes shaped like snarling bears.

Her breath formed into misty angels, who fought the snowflakes back.

She raced into the palace,
through a hundred icy halls.

In a vast glittering chamber,
she found her friend.

Kay,
Kay!

Gerda put her arms around
him. Her tears of joy melted
the ice in his heart.

Kay cried too, and his tears washed
away the ice in his eye.

"Gerda!" he cried out.
"How cold it is here. How empty and cold.
Thank you for coming to save me."

Gerda took him by the hand and together they walked out of that palace of ice.

And there was Ba, waiting to take them home.

Through swirling snow they flew, far
away from the Snow Queen's realm.

Then out of the woods,
came the little robber girl.

"So this is Kay," she said.
"How lucky you are, to have Gerda as your friend."

At last, they reached Grandmother's. She wrapped her arms around them, crying, "Welcome home! Now tell me of your adventures."

Even the roses bowed
their heads as if to hear...

...but we must leave them there, at this tale's happy end.

The *Snow Queen* was first written by the Danish author,
Hans Christian Andersen, in 1844. His fairy tales,
which include *The Ugly Duckling*, *Thumbelina* and
*The Little Mermaid*, are still famous all over the world today.

Edited by Lesley Sims
Designed by Jodie Smith

First published in 2017 by Usborne Publishing Ltd., Usborne House, 83-85 Saffron Hill,
London EC1N 8RT, England. www.usborne.com Copyright © 2017 Usborne Publishing Ltd.